Sun, Sand

By Jenna Lee Gleisner

SPARKS

Picture Glossary

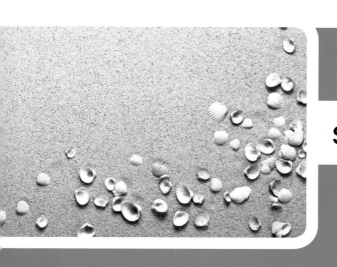

seashells 10

sun 4

I like the sun.

sun

I like the sand.

sand

I like the sea.

sea

I like the seashells.

seashells

I like the sandcastles.

sandcastles

I like the sails.

sails

I like the _____.

sun

sand

sea

seashells

sandcastles

sails

Books, Tapes, and Videos by Chris Griscom

Books

Soul Bodies
Feminine Fusion
The Ageless Body
Time Is An Illusion
The Healing of Emotion
Ecstasy Is A New Frequency
Ocean Born: Birth As Initiation
Psychogenetics: The Force of Heredity
Nizhoni: The Higher Self in Education
Quickenings: Meditations For The Millennium

Video Tapes

Knowings
The Ageless Body
Death & Samadhi
Windows To The Sky I: Light Institute Exercises
Windows To The Sky II: Connecting With Invisible Worlds

Audio Tapes

Knowings
Desert Trilogy
The Creative Self
The Gift of Peace
Death & Samadhi
Sense Of Abundance
Transcending Adversity
Parent/Child Relationships
Ecstasy Is A New Frequency
Psychogenetics: The Force of Heredity
The Dance of Relationships / La Danza de las Relaciones

Dedication

In profound gratitude, I dedicate
"Words of Light" to Allison Ragle for
her unwavering encouragment and help
in creating this little book of quotes.
How blessed I am to know such a
brilliant person who loves words the
way I do and who embraces them
within their holographic meaning;
bringing richness and joy into the art of
communication. Thank You,
Allison!

Acknowledgments

What a great joy it was to ask for help from my children, Teo and Bapu Griscom and witness their skill and knowledge. Thank you both!

Light is the radiance of the Soul

Light is the healer
of all disharmony.
By its power,
we can pass through
any illusions of karma
or places of darknesss.
Light is the giver
of clarity and sight.

As we experience the energies
of the universe within us,
the veils are lifted
and we see clearly
through
the window of truth.
The vision is one of true knowing
that erupts from the Soul.
It may crystallize no images
but for the brightness of light.
If we can hold the flicker of light
until it becomes a flame,
all reality will be forged
through its fire
and transmute itself
into the essence material
we will then shape
into new life.

We are the source
of the hope of the future.
Only the strength
of our consciousness
can create a world in which
peace and wholeness reign.

Peace is the result
of transcendence.
Quiet, sweet, and sure,
peace smiles the courage
just to be.
Peace comes when trying sleeps.

Peace is the gift of the Soul,
offered to the body
to remind it of home.

Choice is the richest tool of all.
With it we can create our world.

The essence of the evolutionary
promise awaits us
in our passage through
the threshold of light.

Inside us, we have
the most profound wealth,
the most profound wisdom
that can guide us in any decision,
in any experience,
into the light,
into who we are.

Your Soul is here
to perceive past the limitations
of your five senses,
past the limitation of the
world around you.

The expansion
of the consciousness
to embrace
multidimensional reality
is what enlightenment
is all about.

Through states
of wonderment and ecstasy,
the ego can expand itself
into an expression
of divine energy.

Where there is no resistance,
there is no harm.

Each one of us is here
purposefully
to give something to this Earth,
to ourselves,
to everyone around us.
We must come into contact
with that purpose,
with the meaning of our lives.
We must begin to see
with our greater knowing,
with our greater God-self,
to understand that we count,
that every single one of us
is doing something here.

Each one of us must awaken
and know that we are
our own teachers
that we are our own healers,
that we are our own priests.

Home isn't someplace else;
home is our frequency,
our experience of light.

Spirituality is our birthright.
Consciousness defines our reality.

Past-life experiences
are seas of vibration,
seas of living energy,
which are still moving
within ourselves.

There are no innocent parties,
no "them and us,"
no untouchables.
The initiation is about
expanding the perceptual field
so that we can witness
the divine purpose in what is so
seemingly adverse to us.

As we spin up
the spiral vortex of life,
all dimensional realities
can move to that quickening
evolutionary process
along with us.
We are dancing
across the membrane
of these dimensions,
across the expanse of the universe
within divine grace.

As a new being begins to grow,
it holds within itself that whisper
of the intentionality of the Soul.

It is not sexuality
that separates us
from enlightenment;
sexuality is an inherent quality
of our Earth experience,
which merges us
with enlightenment.
It is that which allows us
to rush forward
and become the Divine.
Our sexual energy
is the closest energy to spirit.

When the sexual energy lives
within the heart,
we will not have disease,
we will not have confusion
because we will live
its very essence.

You will always be attracted
to something that is going to
create change within you.

The child reminds us that God laughs.

When the Emotional Body
recognizes itself within
the light of the Soul,
it loses its positionality
and heals its judgment.

The more we become conscious
of the hologram,
the more we become God.

Enlightenment knows
the perfection of being
in the center of chaos
and yet
always feeling ourselves
inside the cosmic giggle.

When we clear our former
incarnations,
we are clearing them forever.
We are erasing history!
The Soul is thus able to move
into octaves
for which we have no
frame of reference, yet...

It is only when we have dissolved
enough to experience ourselves
as sound and light
that we can ride the currents of
ecstatic vibration.

Ecstasy soars upward,
fueled by its own momentum,
by its very being,
transcending until it becomes
an energy without a source.
It becomes the Source itself.
This is the source that
creates the worlds,
creates the coalescence
into thought, light and form.

The ecstatic frequency placed
within the medium
of a human body
automatically transmutes
any density of imprisoned energy.

When the hum of ecstasy
interpenetrates life-force energy,
there is a spontaneous
convergence of light
from which springs
the highest octave of divine play
within manifest dimensions.
It is the energy of radiance.

The energy of radiance
cannot be stopped or resisted
or even engaged.
When it bathes the path,
all fear instantaneously
metamorphoses into light.
All separation, confusion
and longing, cease to exist.
Radiance moves beyond the
electrical, the magnetic laws
of the third dimension.
It seeks to attract nothing,
and nothing sticks to it.
It merely pervades all.

The more we practice
radiance in our lives,
the more we will become it.
This is our evolution
back into light.

Each of us
is a masterpiece of alchemy,
a divine blending of elements
that interact with each other
to catalyze a fertile soup
of individual potential.

Feminine awareness
is the precipice of power.
With it, we can leap
off the edge of passivity
into the magnificent,
swirling energies
of the creative force
that transform us from
the inert observers of life,
into the masters of form.

Communication with nature
is an invitation to consciousness.

All of nature
carries within it the imprint
of every evolution
of its many forms,
as well as the actual experiences
with which all living beings
have impregnated
the atmosphere.
All wars, all death,
all laughter, all birth,
echo and radiate out
from the trees, the rocks,
from the earth itself,
as the organic energies
of any place absorb
and hold life
and record its history.

We choose love or the lack of it
by our emotional and
karmic inclinations;
the relationship is not the quest,
but only the backdrop
for the lesson of the Soul.

Competition for love
is an old, outdated thought form
that gives us motivation
for new lessons.

We heal ourselves
by healing others.
We receive by giving.
Within the heart of every human
is a profound desire to give,
to contribute, to be needed.

To apply and illumine
the feminine levels of
consciousness in our daily lives,
we must
draw the formless (knowing)
into interface with the
manifest (doing)
so that
the yin and the yang
can embrace and merge.
At this intersecting point,
energy erupts
from its pure essence of knowing
and is infused with matter,
with thought and intention,
so that it is sculpted into a form
that is recognizable.
That form
is the way we live our lives.

Consciousness is applicable
to every millisecond of our lives,
our survival, our future,
and even our past.
The powerful person simply
holds the energy
long enough to perceive
all the choices that are available
through that particular hologram.

Timing is the dance partner of the successful person.

It is imperative
to take yin energy
out from under
the mystery
and into the mundane.

There can be no true education
that does not encompass
Source.

You have the choice
at every moment
to focus
either on the problem
or on the solution.

True communication
has the requisite variety
of modalities so crucial to success:
how to merge
the head and the heart;
how to dissolve opposition;
how to commune beyond
the mind, the culture,
the language.

As you talk like God,
God talks like you.
This is the power of intention
that actually changes the universe
through you.

If only we could understand
that any demise comes from inside
and that anyone besides ourselves
who is playing a leading role
is doing so at our request.

The mind must be cleared
so that probable realities
can present themselves
via energetic pathways.

It takes great clarity to listen
only to what belongs to you,
rather than to argue
for what your passion insists
you must have.

What we call coincidence
is the play
of the Higher Self
offering guidance
in its own unobtrusive way.

Synchronicity
is the clap of thunder
that startles the mind to attention.

The Higher Self
speaks in shorthand,
not lengthy discourses
on what you should do.
It will not lead you,
it will present you with cues
that can be deciphered
to discover truth.

It is the willingness to engage
that transforms you.

The only way
you can become successful
or arrive at your goal
is through motion.
You have to take a step.
It makes no difference
what direction you take.

What is really important
is the grace
with which you are successful.
If you express with integrity,
every endeavor is successful
because of the quality
of your intention.

If you open your consciousness
to the hologram,
the limitless energy
will nourish you enough
so that you forget
the clutches of need.

You can move a mountain.
You can stop an earthquake.
You can save a tree.
You can call the rain and sun.
You can change the darkness.
You can bring the Light.

The degree to which we can let go
is the degree to which
we can experience samadhi,
or blissful knowing.

If we can see ourselves
in the hologram that laughs,
we can become light.
That is the gift of samadhi.

It is only when
we have dissolved enough
to experience ourselves
as sound and light,
that we can ride the currents
of ecstatic vibration.

The freedom of the giver
is euphoric
when it is unshackled
from the teather of return.

If you can give and let go,
you will experience
a godly sensation
of true power
and mastership of life.

We must realize that the future
can not pass us by.
Indeed,
we are the center
of our own destiny.

The light
awakens our consciousness,
our embodiment
and our Soul.

Once you play with radiance,
all of your control and limitation
and incapacity to quicken
simply dissolve in the face of
the thrill of expansion.

Communication with life
explodes into channels
of recognition
that break the barriers
between species,
between all of nature.

When you step
into the unmanifest worlds,
reality does not rest
upon the small or the particulate.
It expands miraculously
to include infinite
variety and delight.

Inherent in every choice
is the mirror of the self
in which we must seek
to find the face of Peace.

Recognition of spiritual resources
is a new awareness
that will rescue us
from the pit of darkness.
It is spiritual awareness,
that will intercede
in the chaos of the world.

The magnificent sensitivities
of the child
are the guardians of human spirit.

There will always be
the coming and going
of relationship.
Therefore, when relationships end,
they can end with grace.
If you outgrow
the boundary of a relationship,
your partner has the freedom
to expand with you,
leaving behind the contracts
and limitations of yesterday.
At any moment, you can choose
to explore together
completely new forms
of communication and relating.

If you can realize
how your interaction
with the outside world
reflects what you are learning
on the spiritual level,
you will grasp the importance
of contemplation and reflection
as a resource for action.

Through the grace
of spiritual knowing,
we can accept the truth
that we are each our own teachers,
our own healers,
and that our innate wisdom
will withstand the test of life.
The Higher Self waits to carry us
into our Light Body,
heralded by a new epoch
of human consciousness
sincerely willing to embrace Peace.

Feminine fusion,
the merging of all opposites,
is the force of Peace.

Peace comes when there is nothing
lacking or desired.
It is the embracing of all there is,
beyond judgment,
beyond separation,
because it revisits Source.

Though it is full,
Peace is not stagnant;
it moves in the arc of evolution.
It is awake and conscious.

We ourselves
are the only solutions
to our present dilemmas;
you and I
are the goal of the quest.

Time is an Illusion.

When we focus our consciousness
on the inner reaches of our being,
the veils of separation
caught in the tapestry of time
dissolve.

The spiritual body
interfaces with the Soul
and therefore
influences the other bodies
to respond and search out
those whisperings
that access our divine aspects—
even though we are often
completely unconscious
of the goings-on.

We are born accompanied
by the grace
of the Higher Self,
which is not a personage
but an energetic channel
of the unmanifest Soul.

The Self moves according
to cosmic law,
always higher and nearer
the wellspring of creation.
Life moves itself upward,
always toward the light.

We, ourselves,
are the stars of evolution.

Every action or event imprints
itself in the latticework of reality,
not on a time continuum,
but on an interacting
point of synergy,
which shapes matter
in all directions,
past, present and future,
as well as echoing through the
energy layers of dimension.
Thus, any thought,
such as a question,
undulates out across the waves
until it connects
to its counterpart—the answer—
which undulates or images back
via manifestation.

Once we become aware of the
"circular arcing" relationship
of cause and effect,
we will be very sacred with
our questions, our projections,
our desires.

Our bodies have unlimited
perceptual potential
that can be tapped and trained
to carry us across the barriers,
through the veils
into heightened awareness.

We all intrinsically recognize
the rhythm of our own being
and when we move
with that pulse,
we find peace.

Nothing that exists
either as energy or matter
is stationary
because energy and matter
are eternally interlocked
in the blinking beat
of divine consciousness.

Thought forms adhere
to certain strata
of crystallized matter according to
their emotional grouping.
Negative imprints associate
together in the principle of
"like attracts like"
and never intermix with the faster
frequencies of positive emotions.
As they clump together,
they literally form new
but similar realities
out of their very substance!

It is a startling revelation
to discover that thought forms
are not inanimate,
lifeless particles of matter,
but are actually organic,
life-force energies with all the
procreative charge necessary
to produce themselves in kind.
If we become the witnesses
of this phenomenon,
we can participate in the future
by consciously organizing
the energetic components
of our thoughts
so that the new groupings are
of a powerful positive nature
due to the quality
of the source material.

The exploration
of our consciousness
is the most breathtaking
adventure of all.

Telepathy
is simply a
stillness that listens.

We did not choose this game
to pretend ourselves
"wallflowers."

We can blend
with any great being
to increase our scope of truth.

We are not just bones
and blood and flesh,
we are magnificent
conduits of energy that make us
laugh and dance and live!

Your body
is truly your best friend:
a friend who loves you
beyond all judgement,
a friend who will do
anything for you,
and who provides you
with an opportunity
to experience
the sacred pulse of life.

You are a divine spark,
therefore you are enough.
You do not have to change
that divine spark,
you only need to BE it,
to emanate and radiate it.
You already contain
all the wisdom you seek
because you are alive,
and that is the greatest knowing
in the universe.

Detachment
is not about losing the experience
of the thing you desire,
but rather about allowing it
to wash through you
while the velocity
moves you onward.

Like the proverbial
evolutionary tree,
the heart is the only passageway
through which humanity
will progress up to new octaves
of blissful experience
and frequencies of consciousness
that will allow it to fulfill
the mandate of human potential.

This is the planet
of the heart chakra.
All of us are here to learn
about the heart's potential
to lift our spirits up to octaves
of profound human emotion
and compassion.
Through the vehicle
of the human heart,
we can express feelings
that transform
the experience of life.
It is the greatest of human lessons,
designed to teach us all
how to express and commune
through the heart.

Perhaps,
one of the most important lessons
for the ego
is to recognize
that surrender
is not the loss of the self,
but an opportunity to expand
and include new energies.

The secret of peace
is the recognition
of the Higher Self.

If we are to become ageless beings,
capable of wandering
the universe indefinitely,
it will be because we will have
learned to love and honor
physical form
as an expression
of our infinite Soul.

We "forget" our Divine origin. We "forget" our encompassing freedom, our ability to survive any and all circumstances. We "forget" that we constantly enter voluntarily into new learning situations, such as physical incarnation—to attain a single goal: to close the circle again, to return to the starting point of our journey through universes, dimensions of consciousness, and life forms with ever-increasing consciousness until at last we recognize that we penetrate creation, genius. The God Force grows and expands through us!

The Higher Self serves
as the megaphone of the Soul
that accompanies us into body
and allows us to commune
with divine guidance
from our human perspective.

If we recognize
that there are no strangers,
no enemies,
no outsiders, and no "others,"
that all people with whom
we interact, especially our
supposed adversaries,
are souls familiar to us for aeons,
with whom we have arranged
to meet in an intricate
dance of life and death,
then it would be easier
to honor one another
and find more pleasure
in this mutual exploration.

As we develop the conscious
capacity to be the witness
to our interaction with the people
who appear on our life screen,
we begin to actually learn how
to direct the play.

It is we, ourselves,
who make the choices
that design reality.
Timidly, at first, we feel our way
into freedom and responsibility.
The moment we take
responsibility
from the heart
life starts working for us.

Each being we encounter,
even from a distance,
is placed in that synchronous
space
to teach us to reflect on the Self.
It is of great service
to our conscious awareness
to take up the practice
of observing the world
by asking ourselves,
How is this reflected in me?

As we take up the power
to look on the world
and see it as a mirror of ourselves,
we begin to find the strength
to pass through fear
to the other side….
to the shore of Knowing.

Our thoughts move
from their source within us
outward
to become reality.

The healing of emotion happens
when we recognize
the connection between
the unmanifest and the manifest
on an energetic octave.
If we really want to, we can
transpose an ecstatic vibration
from the spiritual realm
into our daily lives.
The opening up of our
consciousness to new perspectives
is the key
to being healthy, whole, ecstatic,
creative, and loving.

All of nature, heaven and earth,
is bent on helping us realize
that we are irrevocably
bound together
as the family of humanity
and must elevate
human consciousness
to an octave in which our
common destiny
becomes a clear choice
that we all embrace together.
The multitudinous catastrophes
that are increasing over the planet
are nudging us to move together
with one heart, one body,
to choose to participate
with the power that each of our
knowing souls
brings forth into body.

Change is imminent
on this planet,
and the catalyst for that change
is consciousness—
easily within our grasp
because it is our very source.

Human creative potential
is unlimited;
with it we can
sculpt the universe.

We are like
the sorcerer's apprentices
who now have
to either
execute a quantum leap
in the development
of our consciousness,
or else
make the retroactive discovery
that we have annihilated
ourselves.

That we might transcend
the limitations of our present lives
is a probable reality
we are fast approaching.
If we are going to alter our genes,
extend our physical horizons,
seek and embrace
the secrets of the gods,
we must give ourselves
permission
to be who we truly are…

The "adventure"
is staring us in the face.
Let us step forward
as fearless beings.
From the dimension of the
hologram,
there is nothing unknown,
unwhispered, unforeseen.
We can never lose life;
we can only be foolish enough
to deny it.

We must open up
the Emotional Body
for the higher, purer,
and lighter vibrations
that do not disintegrate
at the first frown
from the outside world.

By focusing on the deep,
revitalizing energy
of the Higher Self,
we can remember
that we are safe
in the womb of our
eternal consciousness.

One of the most wonderful ways
to heal the emotions
is to use the highest expressions
of emotion, such as laughter, joy
and the childlike abandon that
allows us to feel the ease
of surrendering, bending,
changing.
We are truly the most dramatic
and amusing creatures
on the planet,
and our antics are quite hilarious
when seen from the eyes of the
detached observer.
We need to play.
Life is not so deadly,
nor death so final!

We are untouchable,
indestructible, and even lovable.
Our Emotional Bodies are ready
for the journey home,
hungry for the pleasure
of a job well done.
Let us give ourselves credit
for having played the game
with all our hearts,
as if it were real. We were
magnificently convincing,
especially to ourselves.
The reward is the merging with
our Higher Self,
the awakening of our
blissful, radiant, and fearless self.

You are the all-loving,
all-knowing Higher Self.

We, ourselves
are the point of meaning,
the singular, unlimited
resource of evolution!

The Soul must contain the body.
Drawing its life's breath,
it slips through the veil
and composes the sacred ethers
into a body of blood and chi.

Freed from our evolutionary lull,
we can begin anew
at light speed
to construct a "housing"
that suites
our great human spirit
and our Soul's
wondrous humor.

We talk, you and I,
even when we think
we are hiding.
Involuntary leaps of knowing
pass from one body to the other.
It happens if we want to,
or even if we don't.
But why does it occur?
Am I in your body?
Are you in mine?
How can it pass without a
channel, without a touch?
It travels past time,
through subtle bodies
by means of
consciousness alone.

It is true
that we are one soul family
and indeed,
within the infinite liquidity
of cosmic knowing,
all that you experience
is a part of me
and all that I am
is a part of you.

Water is the maternal sea
of cellular existence.

Space is not the empty void
we perceive it to be.
It is a creative soup,
filled with particles of life
waiting for the impetus
to translate from essence energy
to physical form.

Our bodies are the perfect vehicle
to fuse essence and form.
Their source material includes
all the creations of our
earthly evolutionary ladder,
as well as cosmic designs
from all around our universe.
The greatest possible adventure
awaits our conscious connection
to all the other species
within that ladder.

Experience penetrates form
in such a way as to absolutely
affect the future!

Let the body speak
and it will show you realms
of pure ecstasy and light
and even thought,
at its very source.

Ask where you come from
and your body will spin you out
into the cosmos
and into your absolute essence.

The body wears the mask
of the Soul
and paints itself in the colors
of infinite lifetimes.

Each organ and part of the body
participates in the overall design.
It is the art of the Soul.
All that occurs to the body
does so in conversation
with the Soul,
which allows all,
loves all, knows all.

In truth,
what you do is irrelevant.
It is the consciousness
with which you do it
that makes the difference.

Whatever you resist,
that's what you get!

Your body is rich in
Divine essence,
awaiting your awareness.

You know something will happen,
but you do not realize
that as you are waiting for it,
it is waiting for you!

Indeed, the shaman's heart
should belong to everyone,
that we might feel the life
in all worlds
and bring it into
harmonic helpfulness
in our own.

Soul essence knows
no boundaries.
It does not isolate itself
in the folds of inside and outside,
of that which is not and that
which is. It flows in the currents
of the cosmos and ignites all other
substances with its properties.
It has no beginning and no end.
There is nothing separate from it.
The Soul essence is of infinite
age, size, and shape, eternally
pulsing outward toward new
universes. Between the pulses,
it rests in the sigh of creation,
the ultimate power of birthing.
We are its child.
We are a part of its
all-embracing oneness.

Though the Soul essence
clothes itself in individual bodies,
it never loses the integrity
of the universal web.
The connecting links
cannot be cut
because the core thread is beyond
the substance of matter.

The third millennium
holds a promise
of great joy and peace.
It will not happen around us
or to us;
we must manifest it ourselves.

The hologram of existence
begins and ends in the spirit,
and it is this spiritual connection
that can be used in all its potential
to change our reality.

Speak life, speak well.

Our spiritual heritage
is rich and full
of ecstatic potential
that we have not yet
realized ourselves.

The human heart
has an as yet unfulfilled
and unattained potential,
a kind of power in its stretching
that is felt out into the galaxy.

All that exists, evolves.

As we bring forward
the more enlightened strands
of cosmic encoding,
which offer us the awareness
of our true purpose and potential,
we will no longer seek
survival by force,
but rather embrace
our creative adaptations.

Only when we can view our world
through the clear lens
of spiritual awareness
will we be able to find
peace with all experience.

In the same way
that a negative characteristic
of another person only bothers us
if we are hiding or denying
that same characteristic in
ourselves, what we perceive as
extraordinary and exquisite
is also within us.

We must integrate all that we
know and dream
about our purpose in the cosmos.
We cannot limit ourselves
to the third dimension
and hope to play our part
in the evolutionary scheme.
That which was once considered
impractical fantasy
must now be put to the test
as we practice our true capacities.
We must reach
into the invisible worlds
to pass this initiation
of illumination,
and we must do it now!

Imagine a face of enraptured bliss,
a voice softened
by the expanse of the universe,
a mind stilled
by the infinite sea of oneness.
Imagine that it is you.

The Soul
sits within the center
of consciousness.
If you can feel its breath
upon you,
you will know intrinsically
the purpose of your life.

Consciousness is absolute fluidity.
It is attached nowhere,
yet it is your Source
and you command it.
You can ride the currents
of the universe
through your consciousness
and touch all possibility.

All that ripples in the etheric
flows into us,
and all that happens to us
flows back
into the liquid cosmic sea.
We are not spectators
in a game of winners and losers;
we are the players and
adventurers
in the evolutionary universe.
We are ourselves, the flow.

We are entering into this next
millennium
with a new concept of humanity
and its place in the cosmos.
Not only are we clearing away
the destructive genetic refuse
that impedes our evolution,
but we are now accelerating
the emergence of
a new human species
with a genetic blueprint
that will allow stellar travel
and communication through a
human body more replete
with light frequencies and
cosmic consciousness.

We are not destined to inherit
the weaknesses, failures and
diseases of our ancestors;
we are destined to
help each generation
enhance our gene pool
through conscious scrutiny
of the result of our own
hereditary ingredients.

Psychogenetics will revolutionize
embodiment—forever!

It is time
to begin sorting
through our vast historical
repertoire
and selecting
that which is truly worthy
of future reiteration.

You are a point of reference
to all humans
and that point is not just a concept
of inheritance;
it is a flashing access point
of entry and exit!

You are the very beginning
of a breathtaking dawn,
a whole new chain
of human beings
who will borrow bits and pieces
of who you are
and arrange them in an infinite
array of compositions
that form their Source.

All that you experience
will become your legacy,
a pathway into the future
upon which will walk
a thousand relatives
not yet born.

Just as you have found your way
through the footsteps of those
who came before you,
they will search the meaning
of the prints you have left them,
to discover themselves.

Thought and feeling
define destiny and body.

We are not totally shaped
by a physical world,
but by a more elusive intelligence
of universal proportions
that sketches the conversations
between body and mind.

The sense of freedom
that comes from releasing
unwanted inherited traits
is exhilarating
and by your own experience of it,
you begin to trust who you are.

This is the time on our planet
to stretch all possibilities
so that we can make the leap
into new worlds
that are hurtling themselves
towards us
at Mach speed.

What a twist of fate
that we ourselves
actually
select our inheritance!

The more enlightened we become,
the easier it will be
for us to see the gift
in the irreversible situations
of our lives.

Where once we could
separate ourselves
into different realities,
such as work and home,
now we are reaching beyond
the walls that entrapped us
and are seeking
the freedom of
spontaneous selfhood.

We are in tandem
with all human cultures
and will always be interdependent.
What they felt or do now
creates a sounding board
from which we hear and see
our own lives.
We may not feel that we care,
but we must,
because the flicker
of their experiences
has become the flame
of our potential.

There will not be an era of peace
until all that is past
has been cleared
of unusable particles
and reconstructed
within an enlightened helix.

Humans have been gifted
with more than 70 senses
with which to embrace life,
yet we have diluted
its thrill and richness
by detouring all perception
through the mind.

The goodness in us
needs to be allowed,
without coercion.
The era of martyrs,
sacrifice, and punishment
is over.

There are no
good guys and bad guys;
there is only the lonely human
looking for
the safety of home and family.

Our fate will be
the result of our choices;
that we have the freedom
to choose
is the most precious
of humanity's gifts!

When I discovered
that the gene settings
were biochemical,
I saw the key
to the profound power
of emotion.

We are rising out
of a pit of darkness
in which we saw
only the shadows
of our most urgent fears.
Suddenly,
our conscious awareness
has alighted upon the possibility
that we might find the solutions
to our earthly problems
through the interface
between our limited reality
and the reaches of
cosmic source.

Let us show ourselves
to be capable
of the adventure of change.
The thrill of this next millennium
will be the vast array
of interdimensional
and interplanetary discoveries;
the challenge will be
their application into our world.

We must be careful
not to conclude that we are
the sum total of our genes—
we are not!

Our bodies are not exterior stuff
alone.
They are light and electric-fluidity.
Above all,
they are the form of the formless
and the expression of relativity
that binds us to all humans—
past and future.

It is the Soul
who sets the stage for growth
and begs life to express
its potential
to play out the mandate
of cosmic apprenticeship.

We were given the capacity
to listen to the wisdom of the body
as it expresses the Soul;
to discern through our awareness
the solutions
that will carry us forward.

Our perceptions
are actually genetic habits.
We can make new genetic habits
that allow us to be more available
to what is going on.
We humans
have been in a hereditary groove.
We now have the choice
of dissolving that groove
and all the elements within it
that no longer serve us.

Freed from our evolutionary lull,
we can begin anew
at light speed
to construct a "housing"
that suites our great human spirit
and our Soul's
wondrous humor.

Conscious genetics
is our legacy,
which we will deliver
to future humans
by practicing it now
and transforming our experiences
into the constructs of our physical,
emotional and spiritual DNA
that they will receive
as our contribution to evolution.

We have come to the edge
of the world. We are standing
right there on the precipice
waiting for the whisper of courage
to give us the strength to jump.
If we align ourselves
to the power of change,
we will leave the limitations
that beset our forefathers
and soar freely into a New World.
Change will become our constant
and through its improvisor style,
we will instigate a new pulse.
It will be a pulse that rides
the crest of cosmic currents
flowing outward across
the galaxies, taking the human
heart energy with it to seed
a human being,
we have not yet met!